TWO CHRISTMAS CELEBRATIONS

THEODORE PARKER

Edition : Culturea (Hérault, 34)
Contact : infos@culturea.fr
Retrouvez notre catalogue sur http://culturea.fr
Imprimé en Allemagne par Books on Demand
Design typographique : Derek Murphy
Layout : Reedsy (https://reedsy.com/)
ISBN : 9791041818259
Dépôt légal : Juin 2023

A great many years ago, Augustus Caesar, then Emperor of Rome, ordered his mighty realm to be taxed; and so, in Judea, it is said, men went to the towns where their families belonged, to be registered for assessment. From Nazareth, a little town in the north of Judea, to Bethlehem, another little but more famous town in the south, there went one Joseph, the carpenter, and his wife Mary,—obscure and poor people, both of them, as the story goes. At Bethlehem they lodged in a stable; for there were many persons in the town, and the tavern was full. Then and there a little boy was born, the son of this Joseph and Mary; they named him JEHOSHUA, a common Hebrew name, which we commonly call Joshua; but, in his case, we pronounce it JESUS. They laid him in the crib of the cattle, which was his first cradle. That was the first Christmas, kept thus in a barn, 1856 years ago. Nobody knows the day or the month; nay, the year itself is not certain.

After a while the parents went home to Nazareth, where they had other sons,—James, Joses, Simon, and Judas,—and daughters also; nobody knows how many. There the boy JESUS grew up, and it seems followed the calling of his father; it is said, in special, that he made yokes, ploughs, and other farm-tools. Little is known about his early life and means of education. His outside advantages were, no doubt, small and poor; but he learned to read and write, and it seems became familiar with the chief religious books of his nation, which are still preserved in the Old Testament.

At that time there were three languages used in Judea, beside the Latin, which was confined to a few officials: 1. The Syro-Chaldaic,—the language of business and daily life, the spoken language of the common people. 2. The Greek,—the language of the courts of justice and official documents; the spoken and written language of the foreign traders, the aristocracy, and most of the more cultivated people in the great towns. 3. The old Hebrew,—the written and spoken language of the learned, of theological schools, of the priests; the language of the Old Testament. It seems Jesus understood all three.

At that time the thinking people had outgrown the old forms of religion, inherited from their fathers, just as a little girl becomes too stout and tall for the clothes which once fitted her babyhood; or as the people of New England have now become too rich and refined to live in the rough log-cabins, and to wear the coarse, uncomfortable clothes, which were the best that could be got two hundred years ago. For mankind continually grows wiser and better,—and so the old forms of religion are always getting passed by; and the religious doctrines and ceremonies of a rude age cannot satisfy the people of an enlightened age, any more than the wigwams of the Pequod Indians in 1656 would satisfy the white gentlemen and ladies of Boston and Worcester in 1856. The same thing happens with the clothes, the tools, and the laws of all advancing nations. The human race is at school, and learns through one book after another,—going up to higher and higher studies continually. But at that time cultivated men had outgrown their old forms of religion,—much of the doctrine, many of the ceremonies; and yet they did not quite dare to break away from them,—at least in public. So there was a great deal of pretended belief, and of secret denial of the popular form of religion. The best and most religious men, it seems likely, were those who had least faith in what was preached and practised as the authorized religion of the land.

In the time of David, many years before the birth of Jesus, the Hebrew nation had been very powerful and prosperous; afterwards there followed long periods of trouble and of war, civil and domestic; the union of the tribes was dissolved, and many calamities befell the people. In their times of trouble, religious men said, "God will raise us up a GREAT KING like DAVID, to defend and deliver us from our enemies. He will set all things right." For the Hebrews looked on David as the Americans on WASHINGTON, calling him a "man after God's own heart,"—that is, thinking him "first in war, first in peace, and first in the hearts of his countrymen." Sometimes they called this expected Deliverer, the MESSIAH, that is the ANOINTED ONE,—a term often applied to a king or other great man. Sometimes it was thought this or that special man, a king, or general, would be the Messiah, and deliver the nation from its trouble. Thus, it seems, that once it was declared that King HEZEKIAH would perform this duty; and indeed CRYUS, a foreigner, a king of Persia, was declared to be the MESSIAH, the Anointed One. But, at other times, they, who declared the Deliverer would come, seem to have had no particular man in their mind, but felt sure that somebody would come. At length the expectation of a Messiah became quite common; it was a fixed fact in the public opinion. But some thought the Deliverer, the Redeemer, the second David, would be one thing, some another; just as men now call their favorite candidate for the presidency a second Washington; but some think he will be a Whig, and support the Fugitive Slave Bill; some, a Democrat, and favor the enslavement of Kansas; while others are sure he will be a Republican, and prohibit the extension of Slavery; while yet others look for some Anointed Politician to abolish that wicked institution clear out of the land.

When the nation was in great peril, the people said, "the Messiah will soon come and restore all things;" but probably they had no very definite notion about the Deliverer or the work he was to do.

When Jesus was about thirty years old, he began to speak in public. He sometimes preached in the Meeting-Houses, which were called Synagogues,—but often out of doors, wherever he could gather the people about him. He broke away from the old established doctrines and forms. He was a come-outer from the Hebrew church. He told men that religion did not consist in opinions or ceremonies, but in right feelings and right actions; that goodness shown to men was worth more than sacrifice offered to God. In short he made Religion consist in Piety, which is Love to God, and Benevolence, which is Love to Men. He utterly forbid all vengeance, and told his followers "love your enemies, bless them that curse you, do good to them that hate you, and pray for them which despitefully use you and persecute you." He taught that the soul was immortal,—a common opinion at that time,—and declared that men who had been good and kind here would be eternally happy hereafter, but the unkind and wicked would be cast "into everlasting fire prepared for the devil and his angels." He did not represent religion as a mysterious affair, the mere business of the priesthood, limited to the temple and the Sabbath, and the ceremonies thereof; it was the business of every day,—a great manly and womanly life.

Men were looking for the ANOINTED, the Messiah, and waiting for him to come. Jesus said, "I am the Messiah; follow me in the religious life, and all will be well. God is just as near to us now, as of old time to Moses and Elias. A greater than Solomon is here. The Kingdom of Heaven, a good time coming, is close at hand!"

No doubt he made mistakes. He taught that there is a devil,—a being absolutely evil, who seeks to ruin all men; that the world would soon come to an end, and a new and extraordinary state would miraculously take place, in which his followers would be abundantly rewarded, and his twelve most conspicuous friends would sit "sit on twelve thrones judging the twelve tribes of Israel." Strange things were to happen in this good time which was coming. But spite of that, his main doctrine, which he laid most stress upon, was, that religion is piety and benevolence; for he made these the chief commandments,—"Thou shalt love the Lord thy God with all thy heart, and with all thy soul, and with all thy mind; thou shalt love thy neighbor as thyself."

He went about in various part of the country, talking, preaching, lecturing, making speeches, and exhorting the people to love each other and live a noble, manly life,—each doing to all as he would wish them to do to him. He recommended the most entire trust in God. The people came to him in great crowds, and loved to hear him speak; for in those days nobody preached such doctrines,—or indeed any doctrines with such power to convince and persuade earnest men. The people heard him gladly, and followed him from place to place, and could not hear enough of him and his new form of religion,—so much did it commend itself to simple-hearted women and men. Some of them wanted to make him their king.

But while the people loved him, the great men of his time—the great Ministers in the Hebrew church, and the great Politicians in the Hebrew state—hated him, and were afraid of him. No doubt some of these ministers did not understand him, but yet meant well in their opposition; for if a man had all his life been thinking about the "best manner of circumcision," or about "the mode of kneeling in prayer," he would be wholly unable to understand what Jesus said about love to God and to man. But no doubt some of them knew he was right, and hated him all the more for that very reason. When they talked in their libraries, they admitted that they had no faith in the old forms of religion; but when they appeared in public they made broad their phylacteries, and enlarged the borders of their garments; and when they preached in their pulpits, they laid heavy burdens on men's shoulders, and grievous to be borne. The same thing probably took place then which has happened ever since; and they who had no faith in God or man, were the first to accuse this religious genius with being an infidel!

So, one night they seized Jesus, tried him before daylight next morning, condemned him, and put him to death. The seizure, the trial, the execution, were not effected in the regular legal form,—they did not occupy more than twelve hours of time,—but were done in the same wicked way that evil men also used in Boston when they made Mr. Simms and Mr. Burns slaves for life. But Jesus made no resistance; at the "trial" there was no "defence;" nay, he did not even feel angry with those wicked men; but, as he hung on the cross, almost the last words he uttered were these,—"Father, forgive them, for they know not what they do." Such wicked men killed Jesus, just as in Old England, three hundred years ago, the Catholics used to burn Protestants alive; or as in New England, two hundred years ago, our Protestant fathers hung the Quakers and whipped the Baptists; or as the Slaveholders in the South now beat an Abolitionist, or whip a man to death who insists on working for himself and his family, and not merely for men who only steal what he earns; or as some in Massachusetts, a few years ago, sought to put in jail such as speak against the wickedness of Slavery.

After Jesus was dead and buried, some of his followers thought that he rose from the dead and came back to life again within three days, and showed himself to a few persons here and there,—coming suddenly and then vanishing, as a "ghost" is said to appear all at once and then vanish, or as the souls of other dead men are thought to "appear" to the spiritualists, who do not, however, see the ghosts, but only hear and feel them. Very strange stories were told about his coming to men through closed doors, and talking with them,—just as in our time the "mediums" say the soul of Dr. Franklin, or Dr. Channing, or some great man comes and makes "spiritual communication." They say, that at last, he "was parted from them, and carried up into heaven," and "sat on the right hand of God."

His friends and followers went about from place to place, and preached his doctrines; but gradually added many more of their own. They said that he was the Anointed, the Messiah, the Christ, who was foretold in the Old Testament, and that did strange things called Miracles; that at a marriage feast, where wine was wanted, he changed several barrels of water into wine of excellent quality; that he fed five thousand men with five loaves, walked on the water, opened the eyes, ears, and mouths of men born blind, deaf, and dumb, and at a touch or a word brought back a maimed limb. They called him a SAVIOUR, sent from God to redeem the Jews, and them only, from eternal damnation; next, said that he was the Saviour of all mankind,—Jews and Gentiles too; that he was a Sacrifice offered to appease the wrath of God, who had become so angry with his children that he intended to torment them all forever in hell. By and by his followers were called CHRISTIANS,—that is, men who took Jesus for the Christ of the Old Testament; and in their preaching they did not make much account of the noble ideas Jesus taught about man, God, and religion, or of his own great manly life; but they thought his DEATH was the great thing,—and that was the means to save men from eternal torment. Then they went further, and declared that Jesus was not the son of Joseph and Mary, but THE SON OF GOD and Mary,—miraculously born; next, that he was GOD'S ONLY SON, who had never had any child before, and never would have another; again, that he was a GOD who had lived long before Jesus was born, but for the then first time took the human form; and at last, that he was THE ONLY GOD, the Creator and Providence of all the universe; but was man also, the GOD-MAN. Thus, gradually, the actual facts of his history were lost out of sight, overgrown with a great mass of fictions, poetic and other stories, which make him a mythological character; the Jesus of fact was well-nigh forgot,—the Christ of fiction took his place.

Well, after the death of Jesus, his followers went from town to town, from country to country, preaching "Christ and him crucified;" they taught that the world would soon end, for Jesus would come back and "judge the world," raising the dead,—and then all who had believed in him would be "saved," but the rest would be "lost forever;" a new world would take the place of the old, and the Christians would have a good time in that Kingdom of Heaven. This new "spiritual world" would contain some extraordinary things; thus, "every grape-vine would have ten thousand trunks, every trunk ten thousand branches, every branch ten thousand twigs, every twig ten thousand clusters, every cluster ten thousand grapes, and every grape would yield twenty-five kilderkins of wine."

But everywhere they recommended a life of sobriety and self-denial, of industry and of kind deeds,—a life of religion. Everywhere the Christians were distinguished for their charity and general moral excellence. But the Jews hated them, and drove them away; the Heathens hated them, and put many to death with dreadful tortures; all the magistrates were hostile. But when the common people saw a man or a woman come out and die rather than be false to a religious emotion or idea, there were always some who said, "That is a strange thing,—a man dying for his God. There must be something in that religion! Let us also become Christians." So the new doctrine spread wide; not the simple religion of Jesus,—piety and morality;

but what his followers called Christianity,—a mixture of good and evil. In two or three hundred years it had gone round the civilized world. Other forms of religion fell to pieces, one by one. Judaism went down with the Hebrew people, Heathenism went down, and Christianity took heir place. The son of Joseph and Mary, born in a stable, and killed by the Jews, was worshipped as the ONLY GOD all round the civilized world. The new form of religion spread very much as SPIRITUALISM has done in our time, only in the midst of worse persecution than the Mormons have suffered. At this day there are some two hundred and sixty millions of people who worship Jesus of Nazareth; most of them think he was God, the only God. But a small number of men believe that he was no God, no miraculous person, but a good man with a genius for religion. All the Christians think he was full of all manner of loving kindness and tender mercy. So all over the world to-day, among the two hundred and sixty millions of Christians, there is great rejoicing on account of his birth, which it is erroneously supposed took place on the 25th of December, in the year ONE. They sing psalms, and preach sermons, and offer prayers, and make a famous holiday. But the greater part of the people think only of the festival, and very little of the noble boy who was born so long ago in a tavern-barn in Judea. And of all the ministers who talk so much about the old Christ, there are not many who would welcome a new man who should come and do for this age the great service which Jesus did for his own time. But, as on the Fourth of July, slaveholders, and border ruffians, and kidnappers, and men who believe there is no higher law, ring their bells, and fire their cannons, and let off their rockets, making more noise than all those who honor and defend the great Principles of Humanity which make Independence Day famous,—so on Christmas, not only religious people, but Scribes, and Pharisees, and Hypocrites make a great talk about "Christ and him crucified;" when, if a man of genius for religion were now to appear, they would be the first to call out "Infidel!" "Infidel!" and would kill him if it were possible or safe.

Well, one rainy Sunday evening, in 1855, just twelve days before Christmas, in the little town of Soitgoes, in Worcester County, Mass., Aunt Kindly and Uncle Nathan were sitting in their comfortable parlor before a bright wood-fire. It was about eight o'clock, a stormy night; now it snowed a little, then it rained, then snowed again, seeming as if the weather was determined on some kind of storm, but had not yet made up its mind for snow, rain, or hail. Now the wind roared in the chimney, and started out of her sleep a great tortoise-shell cat, that lay on the rug which Aunt Kindly had made for her. Tabby opened her yellow eyes suddenly, and erected her smellers, but finding it was only the wind and not a mouse that made the noise, she stretched out a great paw and yawned, and then cuddled her head down so as to show her white throat, and went to sleep again.

Uncle Nathan and Aunt Kindly were brother and sister. He was a little more than sixty, a fine, hale, hearty-looking, handsome man as you could find in a summer's day, with white hair and a thoughtful, benevolent face, adorned with a full beard as white as his venerable head. Aunt Kindly was five-and-forty or thereabouts; her face a little sad when you looked at it carelessly in its repose, but commonly it seemed cheerful, full of thought and generosity, and handsome withal; for, as her brother told her, "God administered to you the sacrement of beauty in your childhood, and you will walk all your life in the loveliness thereof."

Uncle Nathan had been an India merchant from his twenty-fifth to about his fiftieth year, and had now, for some years, been living with his sister in his fine, large house,—rich and well educated, devoting his life to study, works of benevolence, to general reform and progress. It was he who had the first anti-slavery lecture delivered in the town, and actually persuaded Mr. Homer, the old minister, to let Mr. Garrison stand in the pulpit on a Wednesday night and preach deliverance unto the captives; but it could be done only once, for the clergymen of the neighborhood thought anti-slavery a desecration of their new wooden meeting-houses. It was he, too, who asked Lucy Stone to lecture on woman's rights, but the communicants thought it would not do to let a "woman speak in the church," and so he gave it up. All the country knew and loved him, for he was a natural overseer of the poor, and guardian of the widow and the orphan. How many a girl in the Normal School every night put up a prayer of thanksgiving for him; how many a bright boy in Hanover and Cambridge was equally indebted for the means of high culture, and if not so thankful, why, Uncle Nathan knew that gratitude is too nice and delicate a plant to grow on common soil. Once, when he was twenty-two or three, he was engaged to a young woman of Boston, while he was a clerk in a commission store. But her father, a skipper from Beverly or Cape Cod, who continued vulgar while he became rich, did not like the match. "It won't do," said he, "for a poor young man to marry into one of our fust families; what is the use of aristocracy if no distinction is to be made, and our daughters are to marry Tom, Dick, and Harry?" But Amelia took the matter sorely to heart; she kept her love, yet fell into a consumption, and so wasted away; or, as one of the neighbors said, "she was executed on the scaffold of an upstart's vulgarity." Nathan loved no woman in like manner afterwards, but after her death went to India, and remained years long. When he returned and established his business in Boston, he looked after her relations, who had fallen into poverty. Nay, out of the mire of infamy he picked up what might have been his nephews and nieces, and, by generous breeding, wiped off from them the stain of their illicit birth. He never spoke of poor Amelia; but he kept a little locket in one end of his purse; none ever saw it but his sister, who often observed him sitting with it in his hand, hand hour by hour looking into the fire of a winter's night, seeming to think of distant things. She never spoke to him then, but left him alone with his recollections and his dreams. Some of the neighbors said he "worshipped it;" others called it "a talisman." So indeed it was, and by its enchantment he became a young man once more, and walked through the moonlight to meet an angel, and with her enter their kingdom of heaven. Truly it was a talisman; yet if you had looked at it, you would have seen nothing in it but a little twist of golden hairs tied together with a blue silken thread.

Aunt Kindly had never been married; yet once in her life, also, the right man seemed to offer, and the blossom of love opened with a dear prophetic fragrance in her heart. But as her father was soon after struck with palsy, she told her lover they must wait a little while, for her first duty must be to the feeble old man. But the impatient swain went off and pinned himself to the flightiest little humming-bird in all Soitgoes, and in a month was married, having a long life before him for bitterness and repentance. After the father died, Kindly remained at home; and when Nathan returned, years after, they made one brotherly and sisterly household out of what might else have gladdened two connubial homes. "Not every bud becomes a flower."

Uncle Nathan sat there, his locket in his hand, looking into the fire; and as the wind roared in the chimney, and the brands crackled and snapped, he thought he saw faces in the fire; and when the sparks rose up in a little cloud, which the country children call "the people coming out of the meeting-house," he thought he saw faces in the fire; they seemed to take the form of the boys and girls as he had lately seen them rushing out of the Union School-house, which held all the children in the village; and as he recognized one after the other, he began to wonder and conjecture what would be the history of this or that particular child. While he sat thus in his waking dream, he looked fixedly at the locket and the blue thread which tied together those golden rays of a summer sun, now all set and vanished and gone, but which was once the morning light of all his promised days; and as his eyes, full of waking dreams, fell on the fire again, a handsome young woman seemed to come forth from between the brands, and the locks of her hair floated out and turned into boys and girls, of various ages, from babyhood to youth; all looking somewhat like him and also like the fair young woman. But the brand rolled over, and they all vanished in a little puff of smoke.

Aunt Kindly sat at the table reading the Bible. I don't know why she read the Gospels, for she knew them all four by heart, and could repeat them from end to end. But Sunday night, when none of the neighbors were there, and she and Nathan were all alone, she took her mother's great squared Bible and read therein. This night she had been reading, in chapter xxxi. of Proverbs, the character of a noble woman; and, finishing the account, turned and read the 28th verse a second time,—

"Her children rise up and call her blessed."

I do not know why she read that verse, nor what she thought of it; but she repeated it to herself three or four times,—

"Her children rise up and call her blessed."

As she was taking up the venerable old volume to lay it away for the night, it opened by accident at Luke xiv., and her eye fell on verses 12, 13—

"But when thou makest a dinner or a supper, call not thy friends not thy brethren, neither thy kinsmen nor thy rich neighbor, lest they also call thee again, and a recompense be made thee. But when thou makest a feast, call the poor, the maimed, the lame, the blind; and thou shalt be blessed; for they cannot recompense thee."

She sat a moment recollecting that Jesus said,—

"Suffer little children to come unto me, and forbid them not, for of such is the kingdom of heaven;" and had also denounced woe on all such as cause these little ones to offend, and declared that in heaven their angels continually behold the face of the Father.

After a few minutes she turned to Nathan, who had replaced the brands in hopes to bring back the vision by his "faculty divine," and said,—"Brother, I wonder if it would not be better to make a little change in our way of keeping Christmas. It is a good thing to call together the family once a year,—our brothers and sisters and nephews and nieces,—we all of us love the children so much, and have a good time. I would not give that up. The dinner is very well; but the evening goes off a little heavy; that whist playing, we both dislike it; so much talk about such trifles. What if we should have a Child's Festival on Christmas night, and ask all the little folks in the town to your nice New Hall,—it will be done before that time, won't it? It will be a good christening for it; and Mr. Garrison, whom you have asked to speak there on New-Year's day, will like it all the better if baptized by these little ones, who 'are of the kingdom of heaven.' Surely little children may run before the great Liberator."

"Just what I was thinking of," said Uncle Nathan; "as I looked at the sparks of fire, I was saying to myself, 'I have not quite done my duty to the boys and girls in Soitgoes.' You and I," said he, rather sadly, putting the locket in his purse and pressing the gold ring gently down on it, "you and I have no children. But I sometimes feel like adopting all the boys and girls in the parish; and when I saw that great troop of them come out of the school-house last week, I felt a little reproach, that, while looking after their fathers and mothers, I had not done more for the children."

"I am sure you gave the town that great new school-house," said Kindly.

"Yes, that's nothing. I furnished the money and the general idea; Eliot Cabot drew the plan,—capital plan it is too; and Jo Atkins took the job. I paid the bills. But how will you arrange it for Christmas?"

"Well," said Kindly, who had an organizing head, "we'll have a Children's Party. I'll ask all under fifteen, and if some older ones come in, no matter; I hope they will. Of course the fathers and mothers are to come and look on, and have a real good time. We will have them in the New Hall. I wonder why they call it the New Hall; there never was any old one. We will have some plain cake and lemonade, music, dancing, little games, and above all a CHRISTMAS TREE. There shall be gifts on it for all the children under twelve. The people who are well to do will give something to buy the gifts for the children of their own standing, and you and I will make up what is wanting for the poor ones. We'll have little games as well as a dance. Mrs. Toombs,—Sally Wilkins that used to be,—the minister's wife, has a deal of skill in setting little folks to play; she has not had much use for it, poor thing, since her marriage, six or seven years ago. What a wild romp she used to be! but as good as Sunday all the time. Sally will manage the games; I'll see to the dancing."

"The children can't dance," said Uncle Nathan; "you know there never was a dancing-school in town."

"Yes they can," said Kindly. "The girls will dance by nature, and the boys will fall in, rather more clumsily of course. But it will do well enough for us. Besides, they have all had more practice than you think for. You shall get the pine-tree, or hemlock, and buy the things,—I'll tell you what, to-morrow morning,—and I will manage the rest."

The next morning it was fine, bright weather; and the garments blossomed white on the clotheslines all round the village; and with no small delight the housewives looked on these perennial hanging-gardens, periodically blooming, even in a New England winter. Uncle Nathan mentioned his sister's plan to one of his neighbors, who said, "Never'll go here!" "But why not?" "Oh, there's Deacon Willberate and Squire Allen are at loggerheads about the allusion to slavery which Rev. Mr. Freeman made in his prayer six months ago. They had a quarrel then, you know, and have not spoken since. If the Deacon likes it, the Squire won't, and vice versa. Then, Colonel Stearns has had a quarrel and a lawsuit with John Wilkinson about that little patch of meadow. They won't go; each is afraid of meeting the other. Half the parish has some miff against the other half. I believe there never was such a place for little quarrels since the Dutch took Holland. There's a tempest in every old woman's teapot. Widow Seedyweedy won't let her daughters come, because, as she says, you are a temperance man, and said, at the last meeting, that rum made many a widow in Soitgoes, and sent three quarters of the paupers to the almshouse. She declared, the next day, that you were 'personal, and injured her feelings; and 'twas all because you was rich and she was a poor lone widow, with nothing but her God to trust in.'"

"Oh, dear me," said Uncle Nathan, "it is a queer world,—a queer world; but after all it's the best we've got. Let us try to make it better still."

Aunt Kindly could not sleep much all night for thinking over the details of the plan. Before morning it all lay clear in her mind. Monday afternoon she went round to talk with the neighbors and get all things ready. Most of them liked it; but some thought it was "queer," and wondered "what our pious fathers would think of keeping Christmas in New England." A few had "religious scruples," and would do nothing about it. The head of the Know-nothing lodge said it was "a Furrin custom, and I want none o' them things; but Ameriky must be ruled by 'Mericans; and we'll have no Disserlutions of the Union, and no Popish ceremonies like a Christmas Tree. If you begin so, you'll have the Pope here next, and the fulfilment of the seventeenth chapter of Revelations."

Hon. Jeduthan Stovepipe also opposed it. He was a rich hatter from Boston, and a "great Democrat;" who, as he said, had lately "purchased grounds in Soitgoes, intending to establish a family." He "would not like to have Cinderella Jane and Edith Zuleima mix themselves up with widow Wheeler's children,—whose father was killed on the railroad five or six years before,—for their mother takes in washing. No, Sir," said he; "it will not do. You have no daughters to marry, no sons to provide for. It will do well enough for you to talk about 'equality,' about 'meeting the whole neighborhood,' and that sort of thing; but I intend to establish a family; and I set my face against all promiscuous assemblages of different classes of society. It is bad enough on Sundays, when each man can sit buttoned up in his own pew; but a festival for all sorts and conditions of children,—its is contrary to the genius of our republican institutions." His wife thought quite differently; but the poor thing did not dare say her soul was her own in his presence. Aunt Kindly went off with rather a heavy heart, remembering that Jeduthan was the son of a man sent to the State Prison for horse stealing, and born in the almshouse at Bankton Four Corners, and had been bound out as apprentice by the selectmen of the town.

At the next house, Miss Robinson liked it; but hoped she "would not ask that family o'niggers,—that would make it so vulgar;" and she took a large pinch of Scotch snuff, and waddled off to finish her ironing. Mrs. Deacon Jackson—she was a second wife, with no children—hoped that "Sally Bright would not be asked, because her father was in the State Prison for passing counterfeit money; and the example would be bad, not friendly to law and order." But as Aunt Kindly went out, she met the old Deacon himself,—one of those dear, good, kind souls, who were born to be deacons of the Christian religion, looking like one of the eight beatitudes; and as you stopped to consider which of that holy family he most resembled, you found he looked like all of them. "Well!" said he, "now ma'am, I like that. That will be a Christian Christmas,—not a Heathen Christmas. Of course you'll ask all the children of 'respectable people;' but I want the poor ones, too. Don't let anybody frighten you from asking Sip Tidy's children. I don't know that I like colored folks particularly, but I think God does, or he would not have colored 'em, you know. Then do let us have all of Jo Bright's little ones. When I get into the State Prison, I hope somebody'll look after my family. I know you will. I don't mean to go there; but who knows? 'If everybody had his deserts, who would escape a flogging?' as the old saying is. Here's five dollars towards expenses; and if that ain't enough, I'll make it ten. Elizabeth will help you make the cake, &c. You shall have as many eggs as you want. Hens hain't laid well since Thanksgiving; now they do nothing else."

Captain Weldon let one iron cool on the anvil, and his bellows sigh out its last breath in the fire and burn the other iron, while he talked with Aunt Kindly about it. The Captain was a widower, about fifty years old, with his house full of sons and daughters. He liked it. Patty, his oldest daughter, could help. There were two barrels of apples, three or four dollars in money, and more if need be. "That is what I call the democracy of

Christianity," said the good man. "I shall see half the people in the village; they'll be in here to get their horses corked before the time comes, and I'll help the thing along a little. I'll bring the old folks, and we'll sing some of the old tunes; all of us will have a real old-fashioned good time." Almira, his daughter, about eighteen years old, ran out to talk with Kindly, and offered to do all sorts of work, if she would only tell her what. "Perhaps Edward will come, too," said Kindly. "Do you want him?" asked Almira. "Oh, certainly; want all the LOVERS," replied she,—not looking to see how her face kindled, like a handsome morning in May.

One sour old man, who lived off the road, did not like it. 'Twas a Popish custom; and said, "I always fast on Christmas." His family knew they did, and many a day besides; for he was so covetous that he grudged the water which turned his own mill.

Mr. Toombs, a young minister, who had been settled six or seven years, and loved the commandments of religion much better than the creed of theology, entered into it at once, and promised to come, and not wear his white cravat. His wife, Sally Wilkins that used to be, took to it with all her might.

So all things were made ready. Farmers sent in apples and boiled chestnuts; and there were pies, and cookies, and all manner of creature comforts. The German who worked for the cabinet-maker decorated the hall, just as he had done in Wittenberg often before; for he was an exile from the town where Martin Luther sleeps, and his Katherine, under the same slab. There were branches of Holly with their red berries, Wintergreen and Pine boughs, and Hemlock and Laurel, and such other handsome things as New England can afford even in winter. Besides, Captain Weldon brought a great Orange-tree, which he and Susan had planted the day after their marriage, nearly thirty years before. "Like Christmas itself," as he said,—"it is a history and a prophecy; full of fruit and flowers, both." Roses, and Geraniums, and Chrysanthemums, and Oleanders were there, adding to the beauty

All the children in the village were there. Sally Bright wore the medal she won the last quarter at the Union School. Sip Tidy's six children were there; and all the girls and boys from the poor-house. The Widow Wheeler and her children thought no more of the railroad accident. Captain Weldon, Deacon Jackson and his wife, and the Minister were there; all the Selectmen, and the Town Clerk, and the Schoolmasters and Schoolma'ams, and the Know-nothing Representative from the South Parish; great, broad-shouldered farmers came in, with Baldwin apples in their cheeks as well as in their cellars at home, and their trim tidy wives. Eight or ten Irish children came also,—Bridget, Rosanna, Patrick, and Michael, and Mr. And Mrs. O'Brien themselves. Aunt Kindly had her piano there, and played and sung.

Didn't they all have a good time? Old Joe Roe, the black fiddler, from Beaver Brook, Mill Village, was over there; and how he did play! how they did dance! Commonly, as the young folks said, he could play only one tune, "Joe Roe and I;" for it is true that his sleepy violin did always seem to whine out, "Joe Roe and I, Joe Roe and I, Joe Roe and I." But now the old fiddle was wide awake. He cut capers on it; and made it laugh, and cry, and whistle, and snort, and scream. He held it close to his ear, and rolled up the whites of his eyes, and laughed a great, loud, rollicking laugh; and he made his fiddle laugh, too, right out.

The young people had their games. Boston, Puss in the Corner, Stir you must, Hunt the Squirrel round the Woods, Blind Man's Buff, and Jerusalem. Mr. Atkins, who built the hall, and was a strict Orthodox man a Know-nothing, got them to play "Break the Pope's neck," which made a deal of fun. The oldest people sung some of the old New England tunes, in the old New England way. How well they went off! in particular,

"How beauteous are their feet

Who stand on Zion's Hill;

And bring salvation on their tongues,

And words of peace reveal."

But the great triumph of all was the Christmas Tree. How big it was! a large stout Spruce in the upper part of the hall. It bore a gift for every child in the town. Two little girls had the whooping cough, and could not come out; but there were two playthings for them also, given to their brothers to be taken home. St. Nicolas—it was Almira Weldon's lover—distributed the gifts.

Squire Stovepipe came in late, without any of the "family" that he was so busy in "establishing," but was so cold that it took him a good while to warm up to the general temperature of the meeting. But he did at length; and talked with the Widow Wheeler, and saw all her well-managed children, and felt ashamed of his meanness only ten days before. Deacon Willberate saw his son Ned dancing with Squire Allen's rosy daughter, Matilda,—for the young people cared more for each other than for all the allusions to slavery in all the prayers and sermons too, of the whole world,—and it so reminded him of the time when he also danced with his Matilda,—not openly at Christmas celebrations, but by stealth,—that he went straight up to his neighbor; "Squire Allen," said he, "give me your hand. New Year's is a good day to square just accounts; Christmas is not a bad time to settle needles quarrels. I suppose you and I, both of us, may be wrong. I know I have been for one. Let by-gones be by-gones." "Exactly so," said the Squire. "I am sorry, for my part. Let us wipe out the old score, and chalk up nothing for the future but good feelings. If a prayer parted, perhaps a benediction will unite us; for Katie and Ned look as if they meant we should be more than mere neighbors. Let us begin by becoming friends."

Colonel Stone took his youngest daughter, who had a club-foot, up to the Christmas tree for her present, and there met face to face with his enemy's oldest girl, who was just taking the gift for her youngest brother, Robert,—holding him up in her bare arms that he might reach it himself. But she could not raise him quite high enough, and so the Colonel lifted up the little fellow till he clutched the prize; and when he set him down, his hands full of sugar-cake, asked him, "Whose bright little five-year-old is this? What is your name, blue eyes?" "Bobbie Nilkinson," was the answer. It went right to the Colonel's heart. "It is Christmas," said he; "and the dear Jesus himself said, 'Suffer little children to come unto me.' Well, well, he said something to us old folks, too: 'If thy brother trespass against thee,' &c., and 'If thou bring thy gift to the altar, and there remember that thy brother hath aught against thee, leave there thy gift before the altar; first be reconciled to thy brother, and then come and offer thy gift.'" He walked about awhile, thinking, and then found his neighbor. "Mr. Wilkinson," said he, "it is bad enough that you and I should quarrel in law, but let us be friends in the gospel. As I looked at your little boy, and held him up in my arms, and found out whose son he was, I felt ashamed that I had ever quarreled with his father. Here is my hand, if you think fit to take it." "With all my heart," said Wilkinson. "I fear I was more to blame than you. But we can't help the past; let us make amends for the future. I hope we shall have many a merry Christmas together in this world and the next. Perhaps Uncle Nathan can settle our land-quarrel better than any jury in Worcester county."

Mr. Smith, the Know-nothing representative, was struck with the bright face of one of the little girls who wore a school-medal, and asked her name. "Bridget O'Brien, your honor," was the answer. "Well, well," said he, "I guess Uncle Nathan is half right; 'it's all prejudice.' I don't like the Irish, politically. But after all, the Pope will have to make a pretty long arm to reach round Aunt Kindly, and clear through the Union School-house and spoil Miss Bridget,—a pretty long arm to do all that."

So it went on all round the room. "That is what I call the Christian Sacrament," said Deacon Jackson to Captain Weldon. "Ah, yes," replied the blacksmith; "it is a feast of love. Look there; Colonel Stearns and John Wilkinson have not spoken for years. Now it is all made up. Both have forgotten that little strip of Beaver-gray meadow, which has cost them so much money and hard words and in itself is not worth the lawyer's fees."

How the children played! how they all did dance! And of the whole sportive company not one footed the measure so neat as little Hattie Tidy, the black man's daughter. "What a shame to enslave a race of such persons," said Mr. Stovepipe. "Yet I went in for the Fugitive Slave Bill, and was one of Marshal Tukey's 'fifteen hundred gentlemen of property and standing.' My God forgive me!" "Amen," said Mr. Broadside, a great, stout, robust farmer; "I stood by till the Nebraska Bill put slavery into Kansas, then I went right square over to the anti-slavery side. I shall stick there forever. Dr Lord may try and excuse slavery just as much as he likes. I know what all that means. He don't catch old birds with chaff."

Uncle Nathan went about the room talking with the men and women; they all knew him, and felt well acquainted with such a good-natured face; while Aunt Kindly, with the nicer tact of a good woman, introduced the right persons to each other, and so promoted happiness among those too awkward to obtain it alone or unhelped. Besides this, she took special care of the boys and girls from the poor-house.

What an appetite the little folks had for the good things! How the old ones helped them dispose of these creature comforts! while such as were half way between, were too busy with other matters to think much of the eatables. Solomon Jenkins and Katie Edmunds had had a falling out. He was the miller at Stony Brook; but the "course of true love never did run smooth" with him; he could not coax Katie's to brook into his stream; it would turn off some other way. But that night Katie herself broke down the hindrance, and the two little brooks became one great stream of love, and flowed on together, inseparable; now dimpling, deepening, and whirling away full of beauty towards the great ocean of eternity.

Uncle Nathan and Aunt Kindly, how happy they were, seeing the joy of all the company! they looked like two new Redeemers,—which indeed they were. The minister said,—"Well, I have been preaching charity and forgiveness and a cheerful happiness all my life, now I see signs of the 'good time coming.' There's forgiveness of injuries," pointing to Colonel Stearns and Mr. Wilkinson; "old enemies reconciled. All my sermons don't seem to accomplish so much as your Christmas Festival, Mr. Robinson," said he, addressing Uncle Nathan. "We only watered the ground," said Aunt Kindly, "where the seed was long since sown by other hands; only it does seem to come up abundantly, and all at once." Then the minister told the people a new Christmas story; and before they went home they all joined together and sung this hymn to the good tune of Old Hundred:

"Jesus shall reign where'er the sun

Does his successive journeys run;

His kingdom stretch from shore to shore,

Till moons shall wax and wane no more.

Blessings abound where'er he reigns;

The prisoner leaps to loose his chains;

The weary find eternal rest,

And all the sons of want are bless'd."